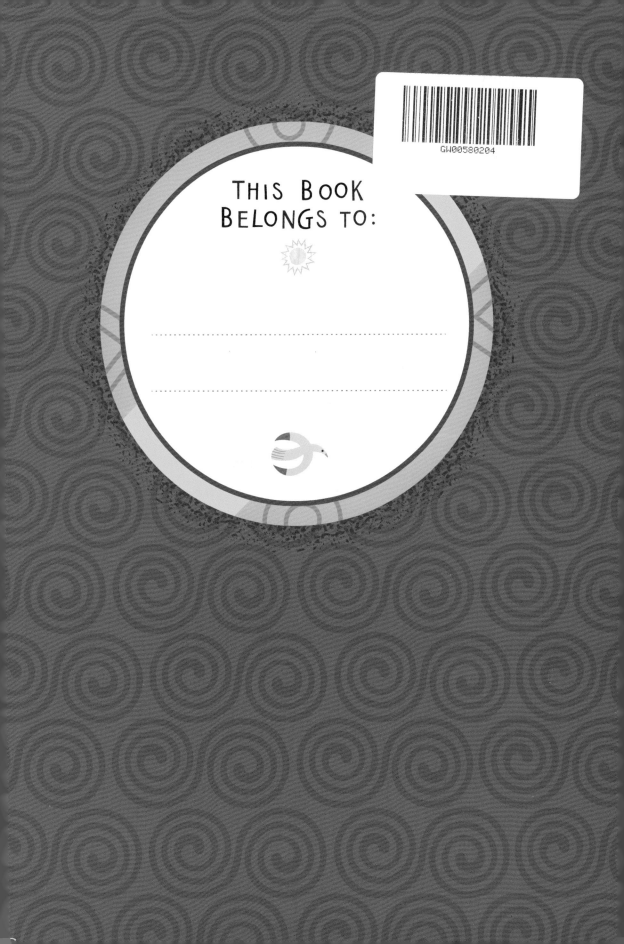

THIS BOOK
BELONGS TO:

GLORIOUS GODDESSES
OF ANCIENT IRELAND

KAREN WARD

PAULA McGLOIN

BEEHIVE

Published 2022 by
Beehive Books
7–8 Lower Abbey Street
Dublin 1
info@beehivebooks.ie
www.beehivebooks.ie

Beehive Books is an imprint of Veritas Publications.

ISBN 978 1 80097 003 8

10 9 8 7 6 5 4 3 2 1

A catalogue record for this book is available from the British Library.

Designed and typeset by Padraig McCormack, Beehive Books
Printed in the Republic of Ireland by Walsh Colour Print, Kerry

Beehive Books is a member of Publishing Ireland.

*Beehive books are printed on paper made from the wood pulp of managed forests.
For every tree felled, at least one tree is planted, thereby renewing natural resources.*

KAREN
To my younger sister Pam Ward – we top and tail our family – who
I watched grow from a little girl who loved to read into a glorious
goddess-like woman who is inspirational.

PAULA
Dedicated to my parents, Anne and Martin, with love.

CONTENTS

FADÓ, FADÓ IN ÉIREANN –

A LONG TIME AGO IN

ANCIENT IRELAND

THE LAND WAS FILLED

WITH MAGIC AND WONDER.

INTRODUCTION

*F*adó, fadó in Éireann – a long, long time ago in ancient Ireland – the land was filled with magic and wonder. Mighty gods and goddesses protected this magnificent island. These powerful deities were guardians of the sun, sea, land and sky. They struck peaceful deals with foes and protected Ireland and its people. These deities had supernatural powers that they used to create storms, calm seas, shapeshift and communicate with birds and animals. They were worshipped and feared in equal measure.

If you look closely at the landscape, you can still see traces of their remarkable deeds – from famous, imposing ancient monuments to the mountains and the rivers that were called after them.

See if you can spot some of these places on the map on **page 57**!

We are lucky to have so many Irish gods and goddesses – each with their own incredible tale. We chose the stories of nine amazing goddesses to share with you, including our matron saint Brigid, who is also a triple goddess; Áine, who shimmered like the sun; and the faerie queen Aisling, who has her own form of poetry. Then there are the Irish maiden, mother and grandmother goddesses – Gráinne, Danu and the Cailleach – who mirror the three phases of a woman's life. Not forgetting Boann, who became a river, and the powerful Morrigan, who could predict when someone would die. Ériu, our sovereignty goddess, was so wise that Ireland is named after her.

These goddesses are like superheroes. Though they are all very different, each of them had a strong belief in their power and ability. We hope you find their wonderful stories empowering.

You'll find explanations of some words and phrases that might be new to you in the glossary on **page 53**.

DANU
The Mother Goddess

Danu (pronounced *Dan-oo*) is the oldest and first of all the Irish deities. She is sometimes called Anu or Ana. Danu is the ancient matron goddess whose offspring were the Tuatha Dé Danann, the Tribe of Mother Earth. Ireland's epic myths and legends portray this race of people as highly skilled in music, culture, science and magic. It is said that they arrived in Ireland in great ships from the sky.

Interestingly, as a key figure in Irish mythology, Danu has no direct stories, legends or myths about her in the surviving medieval texts. The people were constantly reminded of her mothering energies by looking at the beauty and power of nature around them. This knowledge was passed on as part of oral tradition.

As the mother goddess, she symbolises nature and fertility. And it's the land itself that gives us important clues about her character. There are many places named after Danu in Ireland and Europe. The most visible and well known are the two mountains in

County Kerry called the Paps of Anu (also Danu), which look like breasts. She is also personified as the great river goddess Danube, after whom the second largest river in Europe is named.

In some accounts, Danu is described as the wife of the god Dagda and mother to the goddess Brigid. Yet in another story, Danu is connected with Bile, the god of light and healing, symbolised by a sacred oak tree that was fed and nurtured by her. Their union resulted in the birth of a son, the god Dagda.

Danu's name in old Gaelic means art, skills and wisdom. One fascinating theory suggests that because she taught the Tuatha Dé Danann all that she knew, the tribe's name should actually be translated as the 'Tribe of the Goddess of Craftsmanship'.

GRÁINNE
The Maiden Goddess

Gráinne (pronounced *Grawn-yah*) features in one of the most famous love stories in Irish mythology: 'The Pursuit of Diarmuid and Gráinne'.

She was known to many as the maiden goddess and is associated with spring. As a young girl, she lived at Rath Gráinne on the Hill of Tara, County Meath, with her father, High King Cormac Mac Áirt. Said to be charming with a winning smile, Gráinne had many suitors, but neither she nor her father believed any of them were worthy – until they heard that the mighty warrior Fionn Mac Cumhaill, whose first wife had died, was seeking another. Gráinne accepted his proposal, but when Fionn arrived, she was horrified to see that he was an old man and not the handsome youth she had heard about in fireside stories.

Diarmuid, one of Fionn's young warriors, had a 'love spot' – a birthmark on his forehead. When Gráinne saw it, she fell head over heels in love and planned to elope with him.

She put a sleeping potion in the wedding drinks. When everyone but Diarmuid fell into a deep sleep, Gráinne laid a *geis* on him – a spoken spell that ensured he did as she asked. The couple escaped, pursued by a furious Fionn. Later when Gráinne pricked her finger on a hawthorn twig and Diarmuid rushed to comfort her he too fell madly in love.

They remained on the run for years with the support of Diarmuid's foster father, Aenghus Óg, who once hid Gráinne in his invisibility cloak. Finally, Aenghus was able to make peace with Fionn, who then called off the pursuit and married Gráinne's sister Ailbe instead.

Gráinne and Diarmuid settled in County Sligo with their five children and lived happily until Diarmuid died of a wild-boar wound while hunting with Fionn. Old Fionn didn't save him – was it an accident or revenge?

THE CAILLEACH
The Crone Goddess

The Cailleach (pronounced *Kal-yack*) is honoured in Ireland, Scotland and the Isle of Man. The Irish word *cailleach* means 'old woman' or 'veiled one' and *cailleach-hoíche* means 'owl' or 'old woman of the night'. She is sometimes called a hag or a crone, old Gaelic for a wise grandmother. This elder goddess brings in the winter and reigns supreme over the cold months of the year, ageless and immortal.

There are many Irish stories about the Cailleach, who is often described as a pale-faced, wild-haired, stooped, wrinkled woman, sometimes one-eyed and often covered with a veil. Through her association with stormy weather, she is a force to be feared and respected. This protective goddess also looks after those in her care, from humans to particular animals, like cattle, deer, goats and black cats, during the harsh winter months.

The Cailleach has more connections to places than any other Celtic god or goddess. All her sacred sites are wild places that possess her strong energy. The Hag of Beara stone, County Cork, looks like her face turned to stone as she stares out to sea waiting for her husband, Manannán Mac Lir, the Irish god of the sea. From the Hag's Head at the Cliffs of Moher, County Clare, she gazes at the choppy, grey Atlantic waves. As a giantess at Sliabh na Caillí, County Meath, legend has her hopping from hill to hill dropping great stones from her apron to create the many large cairns there. At Sliabh Gullion, County Armagh, the Cailleach tricked the heroic warrior Fionn Mac Cumhaill to retrieve her ring from a lake, turning him temporarily into an old man.

In other tales, the Cailleach lived seven lifetimes, burying many husbands and children before she became a stone and was immortalised as a goddess.

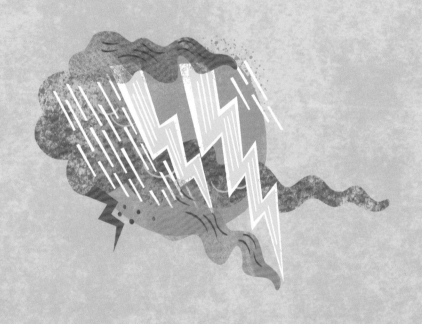

BRIGID
Goddess of Spring

Brigid (also spelt Brigit and Bridget) is a goddess of the Tuatha Dé Danann, daughter of the god Dagda, wife of High King Bres and mother of Ruadhán. Her name translates as 'exalted' or 'noble' one.

Brigid was the bringer of spring in early February at the Celtic festival of Imbolg, a time of hope. Some say she was three goddesses in one, each blessed with fabulous gifts: healing, poetry and smithcraft. The Christian Saint Brigid shares many of these traits. This suggests the use of syncretism: the merging of a religion with an older belief system. The ancient books *Lebor Gabála Érenn* and *Cormac's Glossary*, written by Christian monks, say that Brigid was a goddess of poets.

Saint Brigid is the matron saint of Ireland, equal to but different from the patron saints, Patrick and Colmcille. She is often referred to as Mary of the Gaels. Early accounts agree that Brigid was born in 451 CE in Faughart, County Louth. Her mother,

Brocca, was a pagan slave to her father, Dubhthach, a chieftain of Leinster.

Her attributes were wisdom, healing, protection and blacksmithing. Celebrated for her generosity, Brigid turned water into beer, calmed stormy weather and cared for lepers. She also magically spread her cloak over acres of Kildare's fertile land, now known as Saint Brigid's Pastures, when the local chieftain offered her whatever land the cloak could cover. Her totem animals were two oxen, a boar, swans and a fox that she taught to do tricks.

As both goddess and saint, Brigid is linked with the elements of fire and water. Her traditions are honoured today, including weaving Brigid's crosses and putting out a Brat Bhríde cloth to catch the spring dew. In Kerry, the Biddy – a hay Bríd Óg doll – is a form of yearly protection paraded around at Imbolg, celebrating both pagan and Christian culture. Saint Brigid died in Kildare on 1 February 525 CE at Imbolg and is buried in Down Cathedral.

ÁINE
Sun Goddess of Love

Áine is prounounced *Awn-ya* and means 'brightness and splendour'. Her powerful radiance as a sun goddess ensures bountiful harvests. She is said to be one of the otherwordly Tuatha Dé Danann – the Tribe of Mother Earth. Sometimes she is called Áine Chlair (Áine of the Light), the Queen of the Faeries or the sea god Manannán Mac Lir's daughter. In Limerick, she is known as the Lady of the Lake.

Áine reigns supreme, often with the sun god Lugh, from midsummer to early harvest, as the sunlight ripens the crops. She was celebrated at summer solstice (21 June), when the sun is at its highest. At her home close to Lough Gur in County Limerick – near the oldest complete stone circle in Ireland – she was honoured with a fire ceremony. At these celebrations, people lit torches on the top of Cnoc Áine and herded their cattle by, asking her blessing for a rich harvest.

Sun goddess Áine was sometimes associated with the moon. Old folktales tell of how people came to ask for her healing powers on full-moon nights, known as 'all heal nights'. She was also said to turn into Lair Derg, a swift red horse that no one could outrun.

As a goddess, Áine taught humans the importance of love. In one legend, she married the third Earl of Desmond, Gerald Fitzgerald (Iarl Gearóid). They had a son, Gearóid Iarla, known as the Magician because of his otherworldly powers. When her husband doubted their son's abilities, she took the child and returned to her faerie mound, under Cnoc Áine, to live a peaceful life. Gerald Fitzgerald is believed to live in a cave at the bottom of Lough Gur. Every seven years he rides around the lough on a white horse with silver shoes. Was this a punishment for upsetting goddess Áine, the Lady of the Lake?

AISLING
Goddess of Vision

Aisling (pronounced *Ash-ling*) is the Irish word for a dream or vision. There are many poems and stories called aislings where she appears as an enchanting woman, also believed to be a faerie goddess from the Otherworld, or as a *spéirbheann* (sky woman), who magically appears to deliver an important message. She is a vision of mystical radiance, inspiring all who see or sense her presence to write about her. Her appearance is seen as a sign of hope.

In one famous aisling, 'Voyage of Bran', the goddess charms a warrior, Bran Mac Feabhail, who glimpses her and is bewitched. She fascinates him with tales of mysterious places far beyond the sea. Bran follows her and sets sail with his crew for an incredible voyage to the mythical Land of Women, Tír na mBan. They meet Manannán Mac Lir, the Irish sea god, and discover the Isle of Joy. Each of the men falls in love with a faerie woman and lives happily ever after. But one of them becomes homesick. He returns to

Ireland, ignoring Aisling's warning that hundreds of years have passed, and is turned to ash as soon as he sets foot on dry land. (Always listen to a faerie goddess's advice!)

During the seventeenth and eighteenth centuries, this mythical faerie woman became a strong, inspirational goddess symbolising Ireland's freedom for patriot poets. Their aisling poems follow a pattern: they dream or have a vision of a goddess representing Ireland. She then tells the poet something important and urges them to take action.

Aislings are still written today, and the goddess continues to be an inspiration. As well as in poems and stories, versions of Aisling have featured in songs, in plays and even on the old Irish £20 banknote.

BoANN
River Goddess

Goddess Boann (pronounced *Bo-anne*) literally became the mighty River Boyne, in County Meath. Sometimes called Boand or Bóinn, her name is Irish for 'white cow'.

She was married to Nechtan, who was the guardian of Connla's Well, also known as the Well of Segais. No one was permitted to enter this special place – the home of the Salmon of Knowledge. Nine sacred hazel trees surrounded the well, and the salmon gobbled up the tasty nuts that dropped into the water.

Boann longed to receive the well's wisdom, but Nechtan refused, as Boann was a woman and was not the guardian of the well. But Boann was determined. She walked around the well anti-clockwise, which caused the waters to rise up rapidly.

One legend tells that Boann was punished and died as she was swept along in the rushing waters towards the Irish Sea. Another tells how the well water responded to her amazing feminine power. When she peered deep into the well, the overflowing water embraced her to become the River Boyne, named in her honour. Which of the two stories do you believe?

In another tale, Boann fell in love with Dagda, the father god of the Tuatha Dé Danann, the Tribe of Danu. Dagda sent Boann's husband on a mission. Then Boann and Dagda settled in Newgrange for nine months. Dagda used his skills to bring the sun to a standstill so that nine months seemed like only one day. They had a son, Aenghus Óg, the Irish god of love. Aenghus miraculously grew up instantly and eventually became the guardian of Newgrange.

Nowadays, Trinity Well in County Kildare is the source of the River Boyne. The river flows past Brú na Bóinne, home to the ancient cairns of Newgrange, Knowth and Dowth, built over five thousand years ago.

THE MORRIGAN
Goddess of Death and Prophecy

The Morrigan (pronounced *Mor-ig-ann*) has the ability to shapeshift into many forms, including a raven, an eel, a wolf and a crow. As a crow, she is a foreteller of death and helps people prepare to go to the Otherworld to be with their ancestors.

She is one of three goddesses called the Morrígna, with her sisters Badb (the Battle Crow) and Macha (the Horse Goddess of Ulster). She was said to be the wife of the Irish god Dagda (though others claim this too).

Oweynagat – from the Irish Uaimhe na gCat (the Cave of Cats) – is her special place. This dark cave in the ground in Rathcroghan, County Roscommon, is seen as a portal to the Otherworld. It is said that the Morrigan still appears from here at Samhain, Hallowe'en time.

This powerful goddess had many skills, including encouraging warriors to fight heroically, scaring their enemies and predicting the future.

In the Ulster Cycle's legend 'Táin Bó Cúailnge' (The Cattle Raid of Cooley), the Morrigan meets the famous warrior Cúchulainn. When he defends the north against Queen Medb's armies, she appears first as a young woman, offering him support in return for her love. When he rejects her, she turns into an eel, then a wolf, then a heifer. He injures each of these while he defeats his enemies. Later the Morrigan becomes an old woman with the same three wounds and gives him three drinks of milk from her cow; in return, he heals her fully. Eventually he discovers who she is and apologises for wounding her, and she foretells his death in the coming battle.

After a long fight alone against a whole army, Cúchulainn ties himself to a standing stone, and when the Morrigan lands on his shoulder in her crow form, his enemies realise he is dead, reborn to the Otherworld.

ÉRIU

Sovereignty Goddess of Ireland

Ireland is named after Ériu (pronounced *Air-oo*), our matron goddess. Her name comes from old Irish and translates as 'earth' or 'plentiful', describing Ireland as the 'land of abundance'. In modern times, both Ireland and the goddess are sometimes known by another version of her name: Éire or Erin.

A very long time ago, there were three sisters: Ériu, Banba and Fódla. Each married a king and later became a powerful sovereignty goddess. Ériu married Mac Gréine, 'Son of the Sun'.

When the Milesian Celts invaded Ireland, the Tuatha Dé Danann chose these three clever women to act on their behalf. Initially the sisters demanded that the Milesians go. But the invaders refused to leave. Knowing that they would lose in battle, the sisters wisely arranged to meet their enemies to keep the peace.

The Book of Invasions describes how Ériu chose to meet with the Milesians and their bard Amergin at the Hill of Uisneach, the exact centre of Ireland. This sacred spot was also the gateway to the magical Otherworld.

Through Ériu's courage, intelligence and strength, the sides peacefully agreed to divide Ireland in an unusual way: the Milesians took the world above and became known as the Gaels; and the Tuatha Dé Danann took the sacred sites of the Otherworld below, becoming the faerie folk.

Ériu had one request in this agreement: that her beloved land would be named after her. And so, there on the Hill of Uisneach, Éire/Ireland got its name. The goddess Ériu is said to rest on this sacred site in the centre of Ireland, at the gateway to the spiritual realm.

Ériu received the honour of becoming the Sovereignty Goddess of Ireland; however, Banba and Fódla are still sometimes used as poetic names for Ireland.

THESE GODDESSES ARE LIKE SUPERHEROES, THOUGH THEY ARE ALL VERY DIFFERENT EACH OF THEM HAD A STRONG BELIEF IN THEIR POWER AND ABILITY.

ÁINE

AISLING

GLORIOUS GODDESSES
OF ANCIENT IRELAND

BOANN

BRIGID

DANU

THE CAILLEACH

ÉRIU

GRÁINNE

THE MORRIGAN

GLOSSARY

bewitched	Charmed by magic
Book of Invasions	Also known as *Lebor Gabála Érenn*. A collection of Irish language poems and stories (from the first settlers to the Middle Ages) written by an unknown writer in the eleventh century
cairn	A mound of stones built to celebrate the Celtic festivals and honour the ancestors
Christianised	Christian references, such as to saints, added by monks when recording older stories
crone	Old Gaelic term for an old wise woman or grandmother
deity (deities)	A supreme being; a god or goddess
Earl of Desmond	The titled leader of a place in Limerick called Desmond
elope	To run away in secret to get married
faerie	A different way of spelling 'fairy'
foe	An enemy or opponent
foretell(er)	The ability to tell a future event before it happens
goddess	A supernatural, inspirational woman
immortal	Someone who lives forever

leper(s)	A word for someone with leprosy, a very rare infectious skin disease
medieval	A period in history from the fifth to the fifteenth century CE
Milesian Celts	A Celtic tribe from north Spain who became known as the Gaels after they settled in Ireland
mythology	Ancient stories or beliefs
omen	A supernatural sign
oral tradition	Stories and poems told and shared but not written down
Otherworld	A place where goddesses, gods, faeries, the ancestors and those who die live
patron/matron saint	A holy person who protects a person, church, place or country
patriot poet	A poet who writes positive poems about their country
portal	A magic doorway to a supernatural place
prophecy	A prediction of what will happen in the future
Samhain	Ancient Celtic festival to mark the beginning of winter, celebrated in early November
shapeshift	To change shape magically into another creature

smithcraft	The craft of making things with metal
sovereignty	Supreme power or authority; being in your power with confidence and authority
spiritual	Deep feelings or beliefs, sometimes religious
suitor	A man who wants to marry a particular woman
Tuatha Dé Danann	The Irish for the Tribe of Mother Earth. Ireland's epic tales portray this race of people as highly skilled in music, culture, science and magic. The root of the word *dan* in old Gaelic means art, skill, poetry and wisdom
totem animals	Special animals, usually of a spiritual nature, associated with a person

MAP OF
ANCIENT IRELAND

The magical Otherworld is all around us.

N
W E
S

Down Cathedral

Sliabh Gullion
Faughart

Knowth
Newgrange
Dowth

River Boyne

Uaimhe na gCat
CAVE OF CATS

Sliabh na Caillí
LOUGHCREW

Rath Gráinne
HILL OF TARA

Hill of Uisneach

Connla's Well
TRINITY WELL

Saint Brigid's Pastures

Tír na mBan
(We aren't sure of
the exact location.)

Hag's Head
CLIFFS OF MOHER

Lough Gur
Cnoc Áine

Paps of Anu
ALSO DANU

The Hag of Beara Stone

ACKNOWLEDGEMENTS

KAREN

Míle buíochas – a thousand thanks to the goddesses of Ireland who inspire me to be all that I can be. Now you know why I love to be out in nature so much, hugging trees and talking to the birds and animals every day!

I really enjoyed working with the fantastic Síne Quinn who invited me to write this beautiful book, which is lovingly illustrated by the wonderfully creative Paula McGloin. What a pleasure to work together. I would like to thank Lir Mac Cárthaigh, Pádraig McCormack, Pamela McLoughlin, Leeann Gallagher, Andrea de Angelis Rego, Sean Stilling and all the terrific team at Beehive Books.

Heartfelt thanks to my best friend John – may we continue to laugh, love and listen together always.

PAULA

My thanks and appreciation to the powerful ancient Irish goddesses who have inspired us.

I am very grateful to everyone at Beehive Books for approaching me to illustrate this wonderful book. Thanks to the superb Beehive Books team.

A special thanks to Dr Karen Ward for bringing the ancient goddesses of Ireland to life with such vivid stories – and also for introducing me to new ones that I had not heard of before!

Thank you to Michael for your constant love and support, always.

ALSO AVAILABLE

'A delightful and amusing take on an old story that'll have you humming as you read.'
Siobhán Parkinson, children's writer, inaugural Laureate na nÓg and founder of Little Island Books

'The charming illustrations of Brigid and her fox are the perfect fit for this bouncy legend of a "wee small cloak".'
Margaret Anne Suggs, illustrator of BGE Children's Book of the Year 2016, member of Illustrators Ireland and IBBY

'Rhyme and rhythm, music and song – all in Catherine Ann Cullen's wonderful, inimitable style. What better way to introduce Brigid and her cloak to young readers.'
Áine Ní Ghlinn, poet, playwright, children's writer and Laureate na nÓg 2020–3, the first to write exclusively in Irish

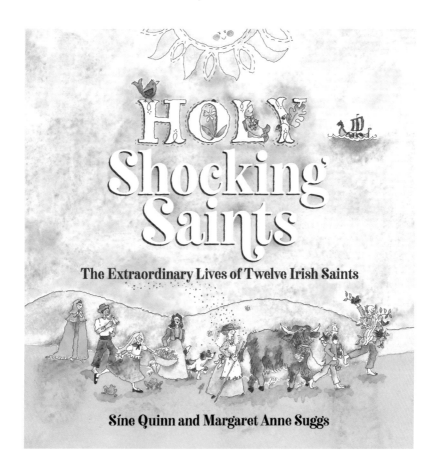

HOLY Shocking Saints

The Extraordinary Lives of Twelve Irish Saints

Síne Quinn and Margaret Anne Suggs

'Author Síne Quinn and illustrator Margaret Anne Suggs bring life to the stories of a dozen explorers, hermits, healers and pioneers.'
Sara Keating, *Irish Times Magazine*

'Explore the myths, martyrs and miracles in this charming new children's book, which features some beautiful watercolour illustrations.'
Michael McDermott, *Totally Dublin*

'Quinn and Suggs work well to create narratives of saints, both infamous and lesser-known, in a fun and engaging manner. This is a great book that will show you why Ireland is known as the land of saints and scholars.'
Ruth Ennis, *Books Ireland*